Short Poems, Long Tales

Big Questions, wrestled with 101 Short Poems

Rashid Osmani

ISBN: 9798718128468

Independent Publishing
Amazon

Other Books by Rashid Osmani:

Word Posse

Pause & Ponder

Last Revision: March 8, 2021

To My Parents...
for giving me their genes.

Contents

Short Poems, Long Tales

Preface

Poetry is hard to appreciate. It's even harder to rate. The main reason is that it's hard-wired to feelings and the intensity of such feelings is different in different people. Even when you take famous poets like Rumi or Pablo, some of their verses create raptures and some leave you un-moved. "Why is that?", one may ask. The reason is simply how humans are created, nothing else. Feelings are tied to receptors in the brain and are linked to sensations or emotions. Even here, every person has a unique range. Not sure who the author is, but that's what it is.

I started writing poetry about twelve years ago. Why I did so is a different story. It's covered in a previous book. This is now my third book of poetry (I cancelled two of them and have included a few poems from them). Hopefully, you'll enjoy some of the poems here.

Bowl of People

And when you look
at a bowl of people
you step back
from what you see.

It may sound a bit arrogant
but the truth often is.
Most of the people
pardon the offence, are a bit idiotic.

Not talking about
the statistical number - that's another issue.
Many of the others
don't have their brains burdened enough.

They believe what they are told
and if it lines up with their instincts
they never let it go
even if it hurts others.

People don't think differently
unless you rub their instincts a wrong way.
Extensions of them leads to racism, LGBT,
and such
natural or acquired, I think.

Piece of Peace

Dark pieces of mind, like black holes
float around
within a mind
to give it no peace of mind.

It's fragile
this peace of mind.
It can't have faith
if pieces are floating around.

It accepts insults
to the brain,
which incoherently
is also the mind.

To hold pieces of mind in place
you need adhesive.
A thought process, like a religion
can work as such.

It's often strong enough
and the mind is not easy to change
when pieces are locked in place.
Hard for non-thinkers.

No Invitation

Deep sorrow flew into my heart one day
and made itself at home.
Being a gracious host
I hesitated to ask how long it would stay.

Sensing my discomfort
it opened up a tad
and said, "I didn't come here
of my own accord."

Did you expect to walk this fine earth
it continued,
partake of its riches,
and leave without knowing my worth?

There is a purpose for everything
that happens, you know it.
If you didn't experience me firsthand
other pains, you wouldn't withstand.

Finale

I retired
because I know
I will die.

Death is known
to everyone else
as an eventual outcome.

But it doesn't register
with depth
no matter how often they're reminded.

It's hard for many people
to reconcile daily needs
with this devastating certainty.

Besides
everyone thinks they're on to something better
after death, and so, they don't dwell on it.

Gender Bender

Is gender physical
and visible,
or mental and invisible?

Visible or invisible
equal is equal, same is same
Equal is not the same as same.

Differences are natural
and visible
bodies are different, yet equal.

May the difference
be more different
and the equal be more equal.

Call Awaiting

My phone,
not used to receiving calls
was startled.

I thought it was you
calling to say you are sorry.

It was an eight hundred number
reminding me of my next flight.

Not Schindler's List

Of all the people
who've crossed my path in life
I am making a list of those
I'd like to associate with
in after-life.

Your name just came off that list.

Our association will end on this earth.
I will not invest any more emotion in you.
Either way
it wouldn't matter,
there may be no after-life for either of us.

Talk Not

Parents often curse
their kids... don't talk to them.
They compare with their friend's kids
and feel worse.

Lighten up, I say.
talking has meaning
when feelings are mutual
and people enjoy the same emotions.

While kids inherit diseases
based on genetics
their temperaments can be way off
with a little change in mentality genes.

Let them live their lives...
Help them if you are culturally inclined.
Our association with them is less in our hands
than we think.

Without You by My Side

While alone and sad,
I do visit your graves
and perspectize my life
as it moves forward
without you by my side.

When living hurts,
death does invite
comforting
with a hidden truth
that alive doesn't have.

We appear one of a kind...
hurting when others we love
helplessly suffer.
Broken families create loneliness
that society can't restore.

Pet People

It's tempting to say
but maybe it's not true.
People with pets
make up for what they don't have naturally.

Who doesn't like love -
Not many
What do you do if you don't have enough?
you go out and get it, unquestioningly.

But the bad part is
Going for a walk
with a bag in your left hand
and a sad grin on the face.

Often, you find them
with a smile
They nod and they say knowingly
their pets are quite intelligent.

Body's Delight

I doubt
if good intentions
of mind
are strong enough
to stand up to
inherent bad instincts
of the body.

All bodies love physical delight.
Very few humans deny this
on one hand.
Human life is relatively short
and much of it is wasted
in ugly side roads
with influence wrapped around.

What's a body got to do
in the little time, it has left
when alone
to understand
that what it's got to do
is what it's
got to do.

Lifting Sentiment

There is a certain firm spot
within our mental framework
that responds reflectively
to what references allude.

Does a mind's hunger
for the unknown create this need...
Or do unmet needs
on display generate it?

The mind is a bit of an unknown.
When reading notes
I realize now, how to lift sentiment from
a collection of words that make a sentence.

Sorry, No Answer

At times, we don't get an answer
for questions that pop up
in our minds.

Mostly, it's about understanding others
and what they think of us
when our own thoughts about ourselves are
a bit jumbled.

Often, it's best to unjumble
and wait for the answer to come by itself
even before we ask the question.

For good news from them, is in a sense
early bad news.
It may be reverse too, but it does not matter.

Dead Body

Isn't it pathetic?
A lifeless morass
quite ready to stink.

It's now nameless.
The form that just converted
to a spirit without structure, now living
in memory.

Civilizations have different ways
to get rid of this waste
Some fair, some foul.

There was a soul inside
some insist
others shrug.

Sad that alive bodies
don't think much about this final form
to make their present living, a little more
pleasant.

Winning

...and let them lose sleep
for losing what they value
appearance, culture, or whatever.
None of which lasts
beyond giving temporary pleasure.

What lasts is goodness
piercing the everlasting Soul
(if there is one)
and that goodness
is no more than to make someone smile.

Endless Endings

The wells are deeper than I thought
the roads are narrower than I remember
Just when I think I know
every way there is to get hurt
I find another one
I'd never met before.

Parting Pains

As you leave my home, I pray
You find joy in virtue
boredom in immorality
patience in adversity,
and humility in victory.

Call me whenever you can,
come home any time you want.
Remember, my love for you
although nearly perfect,
is still less than my self-respect.

Wishing you the very best
from this newly empty nest.

Love, Nonetheless

Love is often painted as forlorn
It isn't.
Make it stand,
but don't let it chase lost causes
where relief is absent.

There is strength in love
especially
from clever people.
They always find a way
if there is one.

Love itself
is pretty strong
and safe.
Unseen it is,
though not a biological addiction.

It's not afraid of death,
nor of time passing by...
It lives its own life...
and has a quiet dignity.
One not always of forbearance.

Under Over-Religious

Oh Creator of a particle of sand
and the entire Universe
You know everything about everything
and more...

Including our hidden sins
the ones we don't acknowledge,
or openly ask for forgiveness.
We hide them even from our nearest ones.

Can you give us the wherewithal
to get rid of them?
Or are they so embedded in our very nature
that ridding them is not possible

I think of the overly religious types
who might have similar issues
They seem to bury them
under the weight of their over-religiosity.

Mental Traps

We all have mental traps:
"Ideas check in, but don't check out".
include the idea of
accusing others of having mental traps.

It appears that there are
black holes in our minds.
Openings guarded by pretentions
Hard to get past them.

Never letting in an alternate view
even if it makes sense.
As if there is a fear of destroying
ideas already in there.

Physical Morality

Laws in the physical domain may have
counterparts in the spiritual domain.
It's hard to understand them because
such thoughts occur within the brain.

When you do see the world a bit closer
you see pain and ugliness behind words
Knowing human nature
we understand that some people misread this.

The real sense is often masked by foggy
nonsense
Emotional statements made out of
expectations.
Religions and beliefs create irritation of not
being agreed to.

When masses of such people get together
intelligence decreases to mob mentality.
Leave me alone, I say
to enjoy the pleasantness of nature.

The future mostly wins if you are alone.

Time of Life

Knowing our own nature
and comparing
with nature of the world, we live in...
A contrast emerges
to value relationships.

Our lives, ensconced in a time
are in ways inseparable.
 Events are never the same
when physically changed
from the time they occur.

We portray pictures and movies
to encapsulate incidents that shape us.
But thoughts and feelings are different
and don't fit in the same memory box
... that stores that brighter past.

Thoughts are Souls

Thoughts capture a mind
and make it do whatever they desire
when they are strong
and the mind is weak.

Mind is vulnerable
and slavish to pleasure, when not guarded.
Some of the Universe's mysteries
enter a mind and look reasonable.

Shortcomings are in details
and temptations are good enough to understand.
Stay within this realm, if you are average like me.
If you go beyond, it becomes hopeless.

Universal mysteries are open to inconsistent flashes
for solutions.
If you are not brighter than average
the unknown unknowns will prevail.

You, Happy?

You have been created
by someone else
You live in a world created
by someone else
It's debatable
if you are an undying spirit
called a "soul"
created by someone else
Perched on an aging body
over which you have little control
You live with people
created by someone else

With all the odds
stacked against you
Do you want to be happy?

Nothingness

Some people ask me
if I have
goals in life

As we emerge
from a nothingness
and fade back into it.

Goals for the time in-between
these two nothingness's
should be nothing.

Anything other than nothing
will fade with time
the bane of our lives.

But life should be lived, regardless.
Pleasing natural born inherent instincts
while not hurting others

as these pain another instinct.

Particle or Wave

Feelings within us
have a biological basis
to stand upon
generated, as they are
by thoughts
self-bred or inspired.

If the rest of the body goes along,
feelings are a fulcrum for action
as the link
between mind and matter.
A particle
from a wave.

Genetic Emotions

After eons of dormant living
in deep recesses of ancestors,
aroused genes in my body
wrestle unfamiliar stimuli

Packets of emotion
from the depths of my being
bubble up to the edge
of consciousness.

I see them surface
and helplessly watch
some lofty ideals
stoop to embrace mundane reality.

I wish my genes were stronger
nobler and wiser
and not spew out weak emotions
that will forever remain unfulfilled.

Timely Time

Sometimes,
time is not for us.
It is for others.

We have to be quiet
and let it carry on
as it normally does.

For some particular periods
time doesn't facilitate changes.
No matter how hard you try.

It does change, though.
Only it knows when it's right
without our say so.

Meaty Beef

I have a beef with the Creator.

If He had to create the universe,
why so huge and complicated?

If He had to create humanity,
why so weak and intimidated?

If He had to create love,
why so fickle and invisible?

If there is no meat in my beef,
why is there beef in my meat?

Ritual

Its perhaps a good idea
to do a death ritual
before you die.

Pretend that you are dead,
who would your nearest relatives call
and arrange for your body's disposal.

How would the mourning look like?
You are gone anyway,
will you be able to look in, and see the pretensions?

I doubt that very much
What didn't amount to much
was amounted to in the end.

...and finally, you're at peace...
without the problems of existence.
That is if you are there...somewhere.

Checking Out

As I keep pushing the cart of my life
through the winding streets of this world,
I start to sense loneliness
gnawing at the heels of freedom I've adored.

As the checkout counter looms ahead
I see my cart fill up with pesky needs
sapping the pride of independence.
And my wallet has no credit for good deeds.

Bragging Blues

I cringe on meeting people
who always have good news
about themselves.

It depresses me.
Makes me feel strangely inadequate
I get angry and disappointed with myself.

I am consoled,
thinking it doesn't matter and won't last
Both my bad feelings and their good news.

Countries are Corporations, My Friend

Inanimate pieces of land
that divide humanity
and arouse
vulgar passions of superiority.

Created and named
to integrate selfish attributes
of inhabitants in a region...
will perish if humanity evolves.

It is frustrating to
live with concepts like this
that take eons to unfold...
when life is so short.

Changing Fate

I know not what is written
about me
in the book of destiny.

I am told there are
only two things that can change
what's in life, pre-ordained.

Prayer can forestall small miseries
here and there.
But the evil eye can cause despair.

To ward off envy's glare,
I keep a low profile
and defer credit for any good fortune.

State of Mind

As I go through life,
there are times when I'm at
perfect peace with myself.

Pictures, look good on media
and success
makes us think that
we've life under control.

Little do we know
that this time runs out, and it will.
We may not
have anything left anymore to show.

Older

When younger
I didn't know I'd get older
With age creeping up
there was nothing I could do to stop it.

Wrinkling body
taught me a few things.
It has its own timeline
and some parts don't quite work.

How come
generations before didn't warn us
about losing this
when our whole life was about gaining it.

Gaming the System

Bad things often happen to me
when I least expect them to.
To keep them from happening
I expect them all the time.

Since their main purpose is to surprise me
this tactic seems to work
To placate them further, I hide any happiness that
comes my way
Let's see how long we can keep this charade going.

I Got it!

For every indiscretion,
there is a gene I can blame.
My choices are all pre-ordained.
What are you blaming me for?

If anything bad happens to me,
it is all your fault,
or their fault
for creating the enabling environment.

The satisfaction
of this explanation
is more important
than the accuracy of its rules.

Getting By

There are plots and sub-plots swirling
around me.

Most have nothing to do with me
but I do need to thread my life carefully
around them
without getting entangled.

Holding my head high at times
or lowering my gaze if need be.

In a world uptight and consumed
by self-obsession, ambition, and pride
Happiness bubbles within me,
but is hesitant to surface
scared of looking foolish and outdated.

I often take the middle road and smile.

Reaching Out

They say my consciousness
is merely a consequence
of physical and chemical
activities of my brain cells
fueled by nutrition from senses
and prodded by memory contents

I demur...

Embedded are tentacles (from another world)
that need no material sustenance
and are active when I sleep
and survive when I die.
They are accountable for my behavior here
linking me to the unknowable and invisible.

Some call it the soul
Others call it the spirit
Some say it's the sixth sense
Others don't acknowledge it
Some call it bull crap.
A few don't even have it.

Chapel Hill Massacre*

As you bury two daughters
and a son-in-law, brother
I shudder to think
what you are going through as a father.

We can never explain everything that befalls us,
but calamities in life
will forever be gauged
with a scale that measured the enormity of your
loss.

May the fragrance of sweet memories
waft over the stench of grim tragedies
Your family paid the price for pervasive hatred
that is fanned to push the fringe over the edge.

* 2015: 3-College-age Students killed by an
extremist.

Solutions with Time

Given enough time
the universe has a solution...

...for every problem there is.
Inevitable, invisible, or impossible.

We can only hasten or postpone
a bit what is inevitable.

We don't see the invisible,
so it may not be there even if we think it is.

Nothing matters in the long run for the impossible
if the run is long enough.

We, the Thinking

We, the intelligent
wise and good looking
can also at times feel lacking.

Then what of those
who aren't as good, obviously.
Do they deserve our empathy?

We, the morally upright
strong and straight...
Should we be forced to accommodate?

We, the rich and well-endowed
when we stoop to meet the others
Shouldn't we expect to be fawned?

Inside of our golden hearts
we have enormous resentment of
unaccomplished people.
Wouldn't it be wonderful if they just weren't
around?

Devolution of Thought

The world we live in
isn't quite as nice as it seems.

Although, I don't follow all norms of living,
I do keep them in mind.

As I interpret,
how deep down emotions act up in others...

Viewing the fuzz of unseen in future
from an anchor of reality in the present

I do question my own imagination
as to how the world might change with time

If evil geniuses rule us
and make it worse.

Drawn In

I get drawn to people
who respect me

For the remaining life
as not much time is left.

Not getting hurt for sure
or feeling bad

Every day, reality
pours a little more sense into us.

Perhaps, it's more dopamine,
or the lack of it.

Prolog of Unseen

All interpretations
of faith or religion
come alive from predicting
reverberations of the unseen.

Some appear to know what these are
and are often very confident.
The rest of us are silent followers
not knowing how to question the predictions.

We emerge from the unseen
live our lives
and disappear
again into the unseen.

Thinking, what do you lose
if you quietly follow?
There is no clear penalty
even if the faith is a bit short.

Gridlock over Wedlock

A divine prescription
for biological procreation
A recipe for domestic tranquility
in an era of chaotic debauchery.

My faith is clear in this institution
acknowledging one acceptable variation.
One man and one woman is the ideal
with exemptions for the exceptional.

I am no judge of other associations,
preferring traditions over innovations.
There is no dearth of naming conventions
more suitable for other combinations.

Digging

A few of us
have rotten cores
and people find them
if they reach far enough
inside of us

Best is to enjoy
other people
before you reach their middle.
Often, it's bad
after that.

Many worlds of relationship
are corrupt
when they end.
Keep it in a way
that yours don't go there.

Balling

We descend, watching
beautifully architected cities
to taste the culture
of inhabitants at a ball game.

The guzzling of liquor
was obese.
as were the aimless, fun-looking humans
long-haired with naked legs.

Dignity hiding in shameless genders
for the most part.
A strand of self-ashamedness asks
Why are you so quiet?

Split Impersonality

As we examine personalities
ours or others
let's not ignore
aspects
not easily visible.

Combinations of agents
released in our brains
triggered perhaps by loneliness
or other lack-lusters
create a dense non-sense
that overpowers real sense.

Left alone, unmolested
this creates animosities.
Hard to disown
after our senses return
with new brain secretions
and original personality.

Doubtful Prayer

I do pray,
but of late I'm not sure it works
though it's required.

Looking at all the good souls around me
(with prayer passion)
makes my less solid belief hard to express

People pray for what has a chance to happen anyway
It focuses their mind and effort
and so it's good, even if prayer doesn't work.

Probabilities give prayers an inside track.
There's likely no spiritual-physical link
and humans are only human, despite some
pretensions.

From time to time, as we live,
we do sense magic that is hard to explain.
Prayers answered may be one such.

Reviewing Suffrage

I've realized
that utter complexity of the unseen…
… and unpredictability of what emerges from it
is too complex for the human mind to sort with
conviction.

Contradictory opinions prevail
large number of followers support different sides.
Depth of stubbornness in beliefs
is an element of the human psyche.

I'm one of them,
breathing, walking flesh with no independent mind.
But, I woke up and had time to think
A straight path without wiggle for myself.

Nothing of the unseen mattered much after that…
… because I couldn't have understood it any other
way.

Lastly, to Last

You know you are on the right path
if there are other paths available for you to
compare.

Dig in the quiet dignity you feel bubbling within
if not leveraged by accidental good fortune.

Alone with endowed good nature, is patience
the only two things needed to survive...

...when possessing a concept of how time passes
as others gaze helplessly in it's wake.

Although, when the real time comes,
you'll find them sadly shuffle their feet...

mumble a few prayers
and leave you alone in the quiet, dark hole.

Contentedness

I try not to go
where I'm not looked upon with favor.
For how many more ailments
can a hurting heart take?

Discontent comes from unexpected places.
It's when what we like is not the truth
and more than often
it does not last for long.

Talk not to me about other broken hearts.
I don't have enough words
left anymore
to go over that again.

Denial

I've experienced
a retrieval, and about that,
I'm reluctant to share.

Lest others consider me a loser
for what choice does one have
when not trusting the Creator?

At an afternoon nap, my soul left my body
and when I woke up
the soul was not sure where the body was.

Finally it did get back in.
Felt my legs stiff with death
before recovering, as I woke up.

Soul seemed fine without the body...

Drifting

Their lives look like dreams to me.
Faith in things they can't see
belief in words
of the improbable.

The solid assurance
of after-life
with a lack of assurance
in this life.

They know for sure
how to deal with bad news.
It's either destined,
or caused by evil eyes.

Thoughtfully

We are thoughts
attached to human bodies
as we live
for a period given to us.

When we die
we are torn away from bodies
and live temporarily in minds
of loving people as thoughts.

Slowly we fade away
with passage of time,
as thoughts are not material
meant to last.

Those who are remembered
are either a naivety concept
of human mind
or an act of invisible magic.

Earthly Meaning of Life

Most intelligent humans
ever created on Earth
didn't quite know the true purpose of living.

Others, such as ourselves
have answers that fit well
within our understanding limitations.

Answers are in closed form
going around themselves.
Not knowing if they are right or wrong

We all do marvel though
at the utter complexity of the Universe.
(microscopic and macroscopic)

Wonderful intricacies of creation
Every answer opens new questions
in a never-ending trail.

The human brain that we host
is the most complex creation, that we know of.
Yet we are at a loss in using it for basics.

Goals

The goal of a Philosopher
is to convince people
that their lives are useless, more or less.

Between the uncertainty of birth
and uncertainty of death
all options in between are unpredictable

Do what you may...
The satisfaction of senses, with pleasure
has no guaranteed future, if there is one.

Outside of a lifespan.

Prayer for Solace

Forgive me, Oh Creator
for misusing your gifts
to enrich myself at the expense
of your less endowed creatures.

Help me give back in charity
what I don't need or deserve.
Judge me by the time I've spent doing wrong.
Reward me for the time I've devoted to worship.

Make the remaining time I have
a period of peaceful detachment
from the vagaries of rivalry
that living on your earth entails.

Away from the ghosts of acceptance
haunting me in a culture
of moral tribulations
taunting your guidance at every step.

Moody

Ether permeates our being
from time to time...

When it does it's moody bit
nothing goes right

If it were easy to understand
we'd have solutions

But it's not,
and yet, it goes away – all by itself.

Enchanted ones claim their beliefs and actions
did it,
but it's a lot more than that

This mystery will always remain a mystery
don't let anyone cheat you out of it by
solving it for you with words.

Body to Mind

When things change in bodies
like the onset of a new disease
Do they ask the mind for permission
to go ahead?

No, they don't.
They are independent
and know that for sure
despite not having their own minds.

It also seems they are autonomous
They behave the way they're built
and once done
they're done.

Un-expected Favors

I present my heart
with artificial hurtful scenarios
to sense its reactions

Surprisingly,
some things don't upset it
as my mind expects them to.

It appears that hidden contentment
is a price of natured goodness
showing up within, where we expect it the least.

Bringing Up

We bring up children
asking them to look
within themselves
and find whatever
they wish to be

You can do anything
you desire, we tell them
or become anything
you wish
in future.

When they actually
do look inside
most find nothing.
Other than idle desires
to please themselves.

It never occurs to them
that we were just lying.
Trying
to please them
with ill-founded wisdom.

Parting

As we've lived together
for so many years
it's not easy to look at the truth
and understand that...

... time never waited for anyone
and it'll not wait for us
We have to sadly accept parting
in this ever-changing world.

If our beliefs are true
we'll meet again
in a place
neither of us knows now much about.

Village in Memory

I'm building a quiet village
in my memory
using good things saved
from various parts of life

Assembling them
in accentuating fondness
with the most precious
starting with you

In the balance of remaining life
any ugliness
gets masked
by retreating in the privacy of my village…

Insolence of Young

Youth polishes spitting virility on skins.
Unknowingly, it arrogates passion

But age does catch up, as we all know
We were young a few years back

Time passes for no reason apparent to us
nature is a slow tragedy, aging and withering.

I don't remember flaunting youth
when I was young, but maybe memory falters.

Wrenching grief envelops with time
the serenity of age would be a poor excuse to
overcome.

Too Much Marriage

Unsure what the bio link is
between being a girl
and her wanting to get married.

Seems predominant in all cultures.
Pathetic in those
where girls are equal but aren't that scheming.

In some societies,
relatively high family smarts
cope up to overcome this.

But even when it happens
future isn't good
if one side is rotten.

Searching On

We look for destinations
and for some its yearnings
for others, it's escape from hell.

I also left home
without defining what I was looking for
at that time

because I knew I'd recognize it
based on
the mix of attributes I had for looking

I didn't find it as imagined
and ran out of energy
to continue looking for it more and more

Only to return home, when done
and find
people I'd left behind had changed

Not all of them
and so I knew
I hadn't changed myself.

Happiness – Parsed

Time is very personal
it moves at one pace
we have a start and an end

If we lose sleep
about the before and after our alive time
all we do is - lose sleep

We parse time
childhood, adulthood, and ending
no period lasts

Success, or failure
does it really matter for time?
one shrinks, the other elongates.

We remind ourselves
of great souls before us
It doesn't matter to them – words don't go where
they are now

The secret to happiness is to
come off the time wrap.
in past or in future
It's now that matters, when alive.

Habitual Addiction

Some instincts force action in bodies
and a few others
warm them up to feel fabulous.

Instinctual comfort becomes a habit
yielding to addiction,
which happens to be another instinct.

Hard to get over this.
Mostly takes the person to death
if clever intervention is lacking.

Words don't go well with addicts
neither does action
Internal change has to occur to overcome.

And how does that happen?
Often, it doesn't
and for many, it doesn't.

Looking Within

Guidance reaches us from centuries ago
well-respected learners
articulate what inspired them.

They observe nature
and how humans behave
well or not.

Looking at their learnings,
we pronounce wise sayings
and no one with sense can dispute

However, the unseen is not in our physical domain
nor is passage of time.
Although it seems that destiny is preset over both.

Convictions

Religions have good lessons
if you get admitted
after the initial hocus pocus

Understanding their rules is easy;
Converting them to
prescriptive behavior is messy

Strong religious people
dominate others
who don't have their own strengths

Real religion's message
is to have a fair reason
on which people rest their humanity

To Soul or Not

Like God,
soul is not visible,
If it were not there,
all will be for naught.

But is it?
Love and time are invisible too
but we see tangible benefits
from them

Not much from the soul
other than dreams
and talk
or is it?

It Said ...

There is a little voice inside me
that says the darnest things.

It said women are little people
with too many private parts.

When the general collapsed today,
it said he must be tired of killing.

It asked me, what would Santa do with 72
virgins?
I said maybe get them all a gift to share.

It went after another group:
If they are so smart, how come they couldn't
avert the Holocaust?

If you renounce the universe,
where would you go?

It said if I don't believe in an afterlife,
I may not have one.

I want to choke the little bastard inside.
It said I could get the death penalty for killing
myself.

Mouthful of Age

It took a mouthful of age
to sense that
a tremendous authority
encompassed
by unpredictability
creates uncertainties...
in this complex Universe.

On the other hand
pondering
at these unending mysteries
we realize that knowledge
was slowly built on itself
shaping our minds as we grow
to comprehend what little we can

Our sustenance,
unfortunately
is dependent on
deep natures and meanness
of fellow leaders
even as we learn
to balance the two variances

It's Only Words

They tell us we were born

We don't remember the actuality
as our brain wasn't working.

They also tell us about life
before being born

Also, about our approaching death
and perhaps life after death
(as kind words of wisdom)

These are all words.

No one has ever seen such things
(eliminating dreams and nightmares)

Words about our living life
tell us of fantastic words of wisdom
by truly marvelous people
from a distant past

Believe them
but don't think too hard if they are true
(It's hard enough to believe today's reality)

Think and harmonize feelings
that arise within you, unwilled.
(They come from where you have no control)

Either way, think.

Enjoy beyond just thinking
how words you listen to
affect your behavior.

Not Heaven

There are so many miserable people
that we live with
It's not Heaven
where they screen them out
and leave us alone

The idea is to be alert here...
The same whisperer is after us too
it's so easy to claim early victory over it,
but the grit in it
has defied the noblest among us.

Three Things

Underestimate your accomplishments
but work hard
to overcome your flaws.

You'll always face problems when you live.
Solve them with knowledge and intelligence
not necessarily from your own mind

If you don't have sense,
you'll be unhappy,
because nothing makes sense

Problems are born
and live in our minds
They die there too.

Gracious Gratitude

When done with all the partying
and indiscretions
our restless heart eggs us on...
We wake up feeling less fulfilled
every time we go overboard.

Looking around and within
my soul is filled with gratitude.
Knowing that I can stay in control.
Of what's already been given to me
based on what went forward from me

Un-Hurtful Love

One sided love
has a backbite.
I've seen good people suffer
in this trap.

It's somewhat magical...
this love emotion
where it comes from, when it does
or where it goes, when it leaves.

Survival
is to detach love
from its tentacles to instincts
that belabors to weakness within

You'll sense its presence, still
and act for the best outcome
of doing what is good, no matter what
Not hurting yourself in the process.

Decent Proposal

After living together for eons
banging away at will
in fornicating sin...

A grand proposal is staged.

With a display of virginal chastity,
and tears to boot,
the coy acceptance is a hoot.

Tragic at Times

Life's nature
is generically tragic.
Not all the time,
but sometimes.

Just look at yourself
or your loved ones
Don't let your eyes or ears
fail the fairness test

We swallow years
one at a time, tragic or otherwise
They go inside our bodies
and do it much harm with aging

A reminder of tragedy is senseless
if no meaning is attached.
Let not the passage of time
go unnoticed without an outcome.

Straight Skinny

I'm not even sure of the things I know
what can I say about the ones I don't?

I re-count my possessions, one by one
even as they deplete, day by day

I've now defined for myself a narrow path
one that'll neither thrill nor put me in peril

My thinking is bounded and folds on itself
packetizing thoughts and putting them on a mantel

Unbeknownst to me, someone pulls the levers
belying the sense of control over what I thought I
had

If mediocrity is an acceptable measure of worth
I've finally reached my goal, despite all my struggles.

Taming of Instincts

We have instincts
(like animals)
But our lives are not run solely by them.

Evolution sharpened the human brain.
Instincts are toned with guidance.
and we have laws for governance.

People lean on them
when they're well controlled.
Internal shame appears when they're not.

Instincts aren't to be trifled with.
See how hard it is to train animals
and how close we are to them in DNA.

Toy Contentment

You by my side
quietly doing whatever you do,
smiling at the iPad.

The TV on mute, castrated
images flailing harmlessly.
Music from the iPod filling the void.

Our phones lying silently
side by side, sniffing the airwaves
for messages of loved ones from afar.

Green tea by you, coffee by me,
with Rumi on my lap in a Kindle:
what more can a soul ask for?

Competitive Exit

There are so many answers I don't have.
Among them is when to stop comparing myself
with others.

When you live, having options is profitable.
Not true when you die.

Because the outcome is not for sure known
despite contentions of surety by many

The garb of potential loneliness also chases me
But aren't we all alone before we come and when
we go?

Compare each other on death beds...
quite profitable as no one wins.

Early Warning

When I was a child, my aunt would say to me
now, you be a good boy,
or there will be scorpions and serpents
waiting for you in hell.

Little did she know
that I'd meet some of them here
and a few would even pretend
to be the best of friends.

Death, on Time

We are an amazing pair
...you and I.

No one can see us
or fully understand us

For you, they have a measure
but for me, there is only fear.

All you do is touch and pass
I patiently wait in place, alas!

No one knows where you come from or
where you go
everyone knows, causing grief is my credo

you are unstoppable
I am immovable

Both of us are very fair
there is no one we spare.

We are an amazing pair
.... you and I.

Enough of Enough

I've eyed the hole up close
and it was deep enough.

I've measured the box from inside out
and it was big enough.

I've estimated the time remaining
and it was short enough.

I'll sigh and I'll smile and I'll shrug
all the way to my spot in eternity.

Disbelief

I limit myself to weaving
with strands of truth
filling the openings in between
with patches of faith.

Not arguing with people of disbelief
nor with those that have no doubts.
I wait for inner and outer experiences
to shed the light of acceptance

There is another world, of that I am sure.
Human senses cannot penetrate
the barriers that cover it
Intellect also bounces off that surface

Cogent revelation
originating from the other side
maybe
the only credible clue.

Attitudes

If future beckons on me
with a smile and a promise
I'm not falling for it
not again, not ever.

I'm going to look the other way
and keep moving on.
Not with pride, not with scorn
but knowing what it did to me in the past.

Isn't it better to carry on with low expectations
and stillness in life?
than be jerked around with ups and downs
and no control over what happens next.

Time Factors

There is a way of factoring in time.

If you look at an old person
you know his time is up
sooner rather than later

And you belittle them,
but not in overly obvious ways
if you are polite

If you meet a younger one
enamored, as you are with their better looks
the time factor eggs you on to be nice

No respect for worldly knowledge
in that young skull.
Yet, some cultures respect it more.

Tongue in Other Cheek

When we, the selfish people
are incapable
of getting what we want
it's called depression.

When you downscale our expectations
to match our disappointments
with clever explanations
it's called therapy.

When we run out of excuses
and still, keep failing
and are tired of blaming others
we use immorality.

Wising Up

Lately, a lot of wisdom
is entering my body
from the internet...

Well intentioned sayings
on Facebook and WhatsApp
try their best to wizen me up

Friends and relatives
compete with each other
to make me wiser

Alas, I remain
as foolish as ever
despite my contrary pretensions.

Parsing Fate

I wondered how they assign
human tragedies from up there.

Do they just get around a table
and point fingers at us?

'Let's make this one a widow'
'Let's give this one some cancer'
'Let's suck the love out of their relationship'
'Let's make them kill each other'

I for sure wouldn't want a job like that
up there.

Leaving Secretly

...and
so we taught them
as best as we were taught
to live a reasonable life

It didn't work.
They had different ideas
and not the smartness
to enable them.

...and so we felt like
leaving them alone in this world
mentally leave
as ancestors left us.

We thought it would be hard.
but it wasn't.
Ideas don't just die with pain
at only our end.

Heart by Heart

The core of my heart
(where likes reside)
does not change with time.

Even when peripherals
needlessly masquerading as love
try to juice it up.

With boundless love
floating around us
in media
Our little brains
connected to our small hearts
get overwhelmed by unutilized vain-ness.

But the heart's core
unlike the brain
is not much desensitized
it seems
for worldly ups
and downs.

Nuance Network

I prefer
fleshy communications.
Not the kind
that obscures organs and orifices.

It took me a while,
but now, I can tell
when you text me
with your middle finger.

Fun not very Funny

My friends tease me...
You don't drink or dance
gamble or do drugs
As far as we can tell
you don't screw around
How do you have fun?

I smile and tell them...
My fun is watching them
do all that
and wonder
why they are still
unhappy.

Sad in Hell

It's not the fire
nor the brimstone

It's not the scorpions
nor the snakes

It's not the torture
nor the pain

What scares me most about going to hell
is that for sure, you won't be there.

Acknowledgments

Poems in this book have been written mostly in the last six-year period. As the reader would note, topics deal with passage of time, love, surprise, and other non-visible aspects of living in the 21st century. Ten poems each from the author's two other books that have been cancelled are also included.

The author gratefully acknowledges encouragement given, directly or indirectly by family and friends as they interacted on a regular basis. A poetry website is also hosted by the author, where some poems are highlighted along with other topics of general interest:

www.osmanipoetry.com

Please feel free to visit the website and leave any comments for further improvement.

Alphabetic Index

	Short Poems, Long Tales
Mouthful of Age	88
No Invitation	15
Not Heaven	91
Not Schindler's List	19
Nothingness	37
Nuance Network	112
Older	48
Parsing Fate	109
Particle or Wave	38
Parting	77
Parting Pains	29
Pet People	22
Physical Morality	33
Piece of Peace	14
Prayer to Solace	72
Preface	11
Prolog of Unseen	58
Reaching Out	52
Reviewing Suffrage	64
Ritual	42
Sad in Hell	114
Searching On	81
Solutions with Time	54
Sorry, No Answer	25
Split Impersonality	62
State of Mind	47
Straight Skinny	97
Talk Not	20
Taming of Instincts	98
Thoughtfully	69

Short Poems, Long Tales

<u>About the Author</u>

Rashid Osmani has been writing poetry since 2009. He has lived in the Chicago area for the past 40 years. More information about him is on his poetry website and on Amazon.